Table of Contents

To the memory of my grandparents, Jenny and Jacob Jacobson, whom I wish I had known, for giving me a living Bible within my aunts and uncles: Samuel, Benjamin, Esther, Ruth Leah and my father, Abraham Moses.

With thanks to Ian, Dan, and Isaac for your help; Ann Cassouto for your editing; Rabbi Maza for your wisdom; and my family, Jerry, Amy and Sheryl, for your patience and love.

About the Author and Artist

A graduate of Brooklyn College, Jacqueline Jacobson Pliskin attended the School of Visual Arts, and painted at the Art Students League. Having taught from pre-school to college level has given her an understanding of reaching all ages. In addition to having served as the art director on a weekly newspaper and a monthly magazine, Jacqueline has written and illustrated many children's books, plus educational material, puzzles and stationery designs, and won awards for her work. Her cable television show, Little Dabblers, is widely enjoyed by both children and adults.

OTHER BOOKS BY JACQUELINE JACOBSON PLISKIN:

My Very Own Animated Jewish Holiday Activity Book
The Jewish Holiday Game and Workbook
My Animated Haggadah and Story of Passover
The Adventures of Simcha the Seal
Simcha the Seal Saves the Shattered Shabbat
Color 'N' Sing - Jewish Holidays
Color-A-Song - Feelings
Color-A-Song - Holidays
Three Plays for the Primary Grades
Cookbook - Congregation Anshe Emeth
Little Dabblers Art Projects
More Little Dabblers Art Projects
The Bible Game and Workbook

MEET B-BEAR AND BENJI BEE

In the woods behind B-Bear's house, two friends plopped on their favorite resting rock. They knew it was funny for a bee and bear to be friends. But since they both loved honey, it seemed really just right.

It was an absolutely beautiful day. They had just run (well, Benji flew) the well worn path from Benji Bee'shive to the rock, in record time. Tired from the run, they slid off the rock and stretched out on the grass.

B-Bear closed his eyes. He could hear the wind rustling the leaves on the trees. He could feel the warmth of the sun on his fur and he just relaxed.

"Oh, this is great," sighed B. He liked his nickname, "B." Benji gave it to him. His real name is Baruch, but Benji thought it would be fun to be called B-Bear and Benji Bee. B and Bee, get it?

Anyway, B listened for Benji's buzzing reply. "Hey, B, did you ever think of how the world got started? I mean, the trees, the sky, this rock, and that we both like honey?"

"You know, sometimes I do wonder about that," answered B. "I have found interesting stories about the beginning of the world and people in the Bible."

"What is the Bible?" asked Benji.

"The Bible is a group of stories about God and the world and people," answered B. "Reading these stories and books helps us to understand all the things we wonder about."

"You mean about the beginning of everything, and all?" "buzzed Benji excitedly. "That sounds neat. Let's get a Bible and read some of those stories!"

"OK," said B, "and we'll start at the very beginning."

Join B and Benji in this book as they read through the wonderful stories of the Bible.

3

In the

The very first story in the Bible tells us of the creation, or how God made the world.

On the first day there was nothing but darkness. God said, "Let there be light," and there was light . God liked the light and called it day. He called the darkness night.

On the second day, God made the sky and called it Heaven.

On the third day, God made the earth and the seas. He made the earth grow beautiful with grass and trees.

On the fourth day, God made the sun and the moon and put them in the sky.

Beginning

On the fifth day, God made all the creatures that swim in the water or fly in the sky.

On the sixth day, God made the animals, big and small, to walk on the earth, even tiny creeping bugs. Then God made a man "in His image," to rule over all the creatures in the seas, on land and in the sky. God was pleased with all the good things He created and blessed them all.

On the seventh day, God rested from all the work. God blessed this day as the day of rest.

What is it?

Color the different areas to find a full picture. Use the guide below. What do you see in the picture?

• Yellow ▪ Orange
▲ Pink

6

Baruch and Benji's
wordsearch #1

```
H T R A E A S Q S L G P Z A Y N H J
S I G R J N U U H O I O A F G R E L
B S N D O I N B X C S G E C X I A F
I E J N D M N O O M S A H B X C V L
N S A A W A U D U I G K E T X G E T
M E S R M L V Y V S U A Y S O Y N B
O V O B H S P N H T S W D F X Z J I
Y E A Y S T O R I E S S O A Y S A B
C E B T E F C A Q B O O Z K F X O L
Z B H O A I X I Q A U Z Y W Q M R E
Y V E U G R D J G C W U P E E B Y W
```

Find these words in the letters above.

BEE	LIGHT	HEAVEN
BEAR	SUN	EARTH
BIBLE	MOON	SEAS
STORIES	SKY	ANIMALS

Can you put these words in abc order?

7

ADAM
in the Garden

Adam and Eve were the first man and woman. God made Adam and put him in the Garden of Eden to live. The Garden of Eden was very beautiful, with trees and fruit to eat. There were two very special trees, called the Tree of Life and the Tree of Knowledge of Good and Bad. God told Adam that he could eat thefruit of any of the trees in the Garden except for the Tree of Knowledge, or he would die.

Adam named all the animals. Everything was beautiful in the Garden, but even with all the animals around, Adam felt lonely. He needed to be with another human being like himself. God saw this and understood. God put Adam to sleep, took one of Adam's ribs and made a woman. Now there was Eve.

Adam and Eve lived happily in the Garden and obeyed God. But there was an evil serpent, or snake there. The snake knew about the Tree of Knowledge, and planned evil. The serpent told Eve that he thought it would be great to taste the apple he had picked from the Tree of Knowledge. That nasty snake got Eve to bite into the apple. Nothing happened, so Eve took the apple to Adam.

"Look, I ate a piece of the apple. Come on, Adam, try it," coaxed Eve. Adam decided that he might as well try it. After all, nothing happened to Eve. So he took the apple and ate it.

Suddenly Adam and Eve felt guilty. They had done something bad.

EVE

God called them and they tried to hide. They admitted that they had eaten the forbidden fruit. Adam said that Eve gave it to him, and Eve told God that the serpent made her eat it, so they were all punished.

God made the serpent crawl on his tummy and eat dirt. He made Adam and Eve leave the Garden. Life would be very hard from that time on. They would feel pain, grow old and die instead of living forever.

Cain & Abel

Adam and Eve had two sons, Cain and Abel. Cain grew food in the earth and Abel cared for the sheep and other animals. They both made offerings to God, but Cain saw that God liked Abel's offering better. This made Cain jealous of Abel. One day Cain was so angry that he hit his brother Abel and killed him. God asked Cain where his brother Abel was. To cover up his terrible deed, Cain asked, "Am I my brother's keeper?" pretending that he knew nothing. By his answer God knew what had happened. For punishment, Cain was sent away, to travel all over the earth. Cain said he was afraid someone would kill him for his bad deed, so God put a mark on his forehead to protect him.

After awhile, Adam and Eve had a son named Seth, and many more children. But that's another story.

9

Connect the dots to find out what caused Adam and Eve a lot of trouble. Then have fun coloring.

BENJI'S

TRIVIA Quiz

QUESTIONS

(clues on pages 4,5,8,9)

1. How many days did God work to make the world?
2. What did God do on the seventh day?
3. What is the name of the first man?
4. What is the name of the first woman?
5. What did God make man from?
6. What did God use to make woman?
7. Where did Adam and Eve live?
8. Who gave Eve the forbidden fruit?
9. What happened to the serpent for his sin?
10. What happened to Adam and Eve for eating the apple?
11. What tree did the forbidden fruit come from?
12. What were the names of Adam and Eve's first two sons?
13. Who killed his brother and why?
14. What was Cain's punishment?
15. What did God do to protect Cain?

ANSWERS:

1) Six
2) Rested
3) Adam
4) Eve
5) Clay or earth
6) One of Adam's ribs.
7) The Garden of Eden
8) The serpent
9) He was made to crawl on his belly and eat dirt
10) They were sent out of the Garden and had to work hard, feel pain and not live forever.
11) Tree of Knowledge
12) Cain and Abel.
13) Cain was jealous of Abel
14) To travel the earth
15) Put a mark on his forehead

11

NOAH

Many years after Adam and Eve, the world was filled with people. But they were very bad and God was unhappy. There was only one man who lived a good life. His name was Noah. Noah had three sons, Shem, Ham and Japheth.

God told Noah that the world was filled with so much wickedness that He would destroy it all with a big flood. Everyone but Noah and his family would be destroyed. Noah was told to build an ark. So, Noah and his sons built a big ark.

They put two of every animal on the earth into the ark. Two cats, two dogs, two lions, two zebras, two elephants, two mice, two cockroaches, two beetles, two snakes, two doves, two hawks well, you just name them, they had them. Two of everything, a male and a female.

When all the animals and Noah and his sons and their wives and children were all on the ark, it started to rain. It rained and rained and rained. It rained for forty days and forty nights. The land was covered with water and all living things drowned in the huge flood, except Noah, his

and the ARK

family and the animals on the ark.

The ark floated in the water for 150 days. Noah sent out a dove to see if there was land, but the dove came back. Seven days later, Noah sent the dove out again and this time it came back with an olive branch. This meant that the water was leaving the land. After seven more days, he again sent out the dove, but this time it did not return. Now Noah knew that the earth was dry.

Everyone left the ark. Noah made an offering to God. Now Noah's family would fill the earth with people. God promised never again to flood the world, and as a sign, He put a rainbow in the sky. And so, whenever it rains we see a rainbow in the sky as a reminder of God'spromise to Noah and all of us.

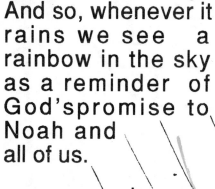

Find your way through the maze of animals and rooms on the ark until you find Noah's room. Enter through the door.

Hidden Pictures

Color the different areas to find a full picture.

Use the guide below. What do you see in the picture?

R- Red   Y- Yellow   G- Green   A- Blue   O- Orange   B- Brown

15

The Tower of Babel

After the flood, Noah and his family had children. Their children had children. Then their children's children had children until there were many, many people on the earth.

These people all spoke the same language. They also felt very, very smart. The people got a great idea. They would build a tower. A tower so high that it would reach all the way up to heaven. There was no limit to what they thought they could do.

They began building the tower. Oh, they felt so smart. The problem was that they thought they could be smarter than God. Well, God saw what these people were doing and He did not like it. God wanted to stop them from building the tower. So He decided to confuse them.

The people worked very well together. Everyone understood each other because they all spoke the same language. Then, suddenly, when one person talked, the other person did not understand him. What was happening? No one could understand anyone. They were all talking in different languages. Everyone was babbeling and no work could be done. Everyone was confused. That is why the tower is called the Tower of Babel.

Work on the tower was stopped. People went off into many groups. Each group spoke a different language. That was the start of all the different languages of the world.

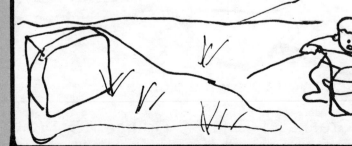

BARUCH'S Word Puzzle

(Clues on pages 4-5, 8-9, 12-13, 16)

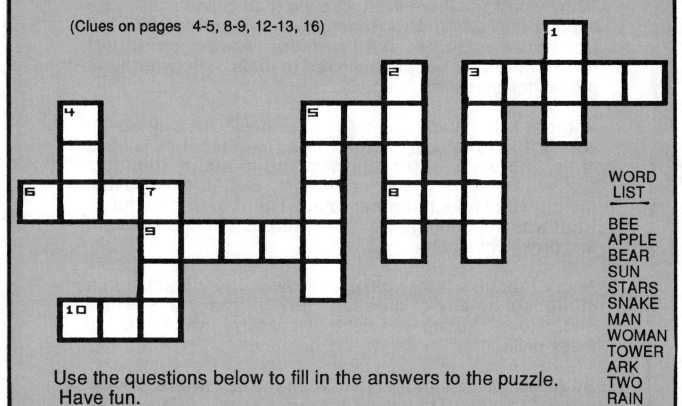

WORD LIST

BEE
APPLE
BEAR
SUN
STARS
SNAKE
MAN
WOMAN
TOWER
ARK
TWO
RAIN

Use the questions below to fill in the answers to the puzzle. Have fun.

Across	Down
3. ☆ ☆ ☆	1. (man)
5. 1 + 1 = ___	2. (woman)
6. (bear) 8. (ark/boat)	3. (snake) 4. (bee)
9. (apple) 10. ☀	5. (tower)
	7. (rain)

17

ABRAM the IDOLS

Many years ago there lived a young man called Abram. He lived in the town of Ur. People there prayed to idols, but not Abram. He believed in God. Abram could not understand why people believed in idols. He wanted to prove that idols were not gods.

Abram's father made and sold stone idols. One day Abram was left to take care of the store. He smashed all the idols. Abram's father returned and found all the idols broken. Hewas very angry at Abram. But Abram said that the biggest idol hit another idol. Then, before he knew what was happening, the other statues got into the fight and broke one another.

Angry, Abram's father asked: "How in the world could a stone idol do any of those things?" Finally, his father understood. Abram was right. How silly it was to pray to these dolls.

So Abram, his father and family left the city where people prayed to idols. They lived for many happy years in the land of Haran. There they worshiped the true God. After Abram's father died, God told him to leave his father's house. God would bring him to a new place to live. Now God promised to make Abram the father of a new nation.

Abram with his wife, Sarai, and his nephew, Lot, had to travel a long time. Finally, they reached Canaan, the land God had promised to Abram and all his future families. Then God told Abram to look up and count the stars in the sky. That would be how many children he would have many, many more than he could count.

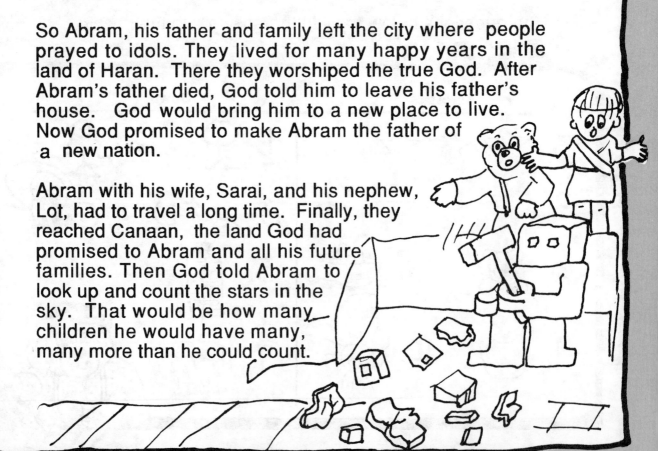

Baruch and Benji's 2nd Wordsearch

```
V M F U X Q P Y V K T B V C R J O E
Y V R I C S Q H E W T W O A B B B U
A D U J M P I Y J S F W J D A G S F
R I I A I S S G M Y N Q F A B T R F
K V T H B N R D A U M F S M E O T V
U U L A A E I K D F E V E K L Y O S
E L P P A O L A A D E Y B H Y M W S
K L S B I X N N R W U E E T Q T E O
Z L T A R O S B T K A L R F V C R I
R X V Q T P C A I N S H Z T M R F Q
T Y M A U U C I D O L S Z O T K N B
```

FIND THESE WORDS IN THE LETTERS ABOVE:

ADAM
EVE
TREE
FRUIT
APPLE

CAIN
ABEL
NOAH
ARK
TWO

RAIN
BABEL
TOWER
IDOLS
PRAY
SKY

19

ABRAHAM...A

God had promised that Abram would be the father of a large nation. How could this be? Abram and Sarai had no children. So Abram also married Sarai's servant, Hagar. She gave him his first child, a son, Ismael.

Later, God changed Abram's name to Abraham. Sarai would be called Sarah. God said that they would have a son. He would keep His promise with Abraham through their son. The days passed and Abraham sat in his tent. He saw three men walking in the desert. Abraham ran out to meet them. He gave them food. Abraham gave them water to wash their hot feet. Then they rested in the shade. These men were God and two angels in disguise. They told Abraham that Sarah would have a child. She heard them and laughed to herself. She was too old to have a baby. But God heard her laugh and said, "Isaac means laughter. You will have a son and call him Isaac."

As the men left, God told Abraham that

NEW NAME

they were going to the cities of Sodom and Gomorroh. The people of those cities were so evil that God could not let them live. Abraham's nephew, Lot, lived in Sodom. Abraham pleaded with God to save the cities. "Would you destroy the good as well as the evil?" questioned Abraham. God agreed that if He found fifty good men He would save the city. Then Abraham begged God to save the city if there were only forty good men. And God agreed. Then if there were only thirty good men. Then twenty good men. Finally, Abraham pleaded to save the city for only ten good men. Again God agreed, but the city would be saved for no less than ten.

God did not find even ten good men in Sodom. Only Lot and his family were good people. The angels quickly pulled Lot, his wife and two daughters out of Sodom. Outside the city, the angels said, "Run and do not look back." As they ran, God destroyed the cities with fire from the sky. But Lot's wife disobeyed and turned to look back at the cities. As she turned around, she turned into a statue of salt.

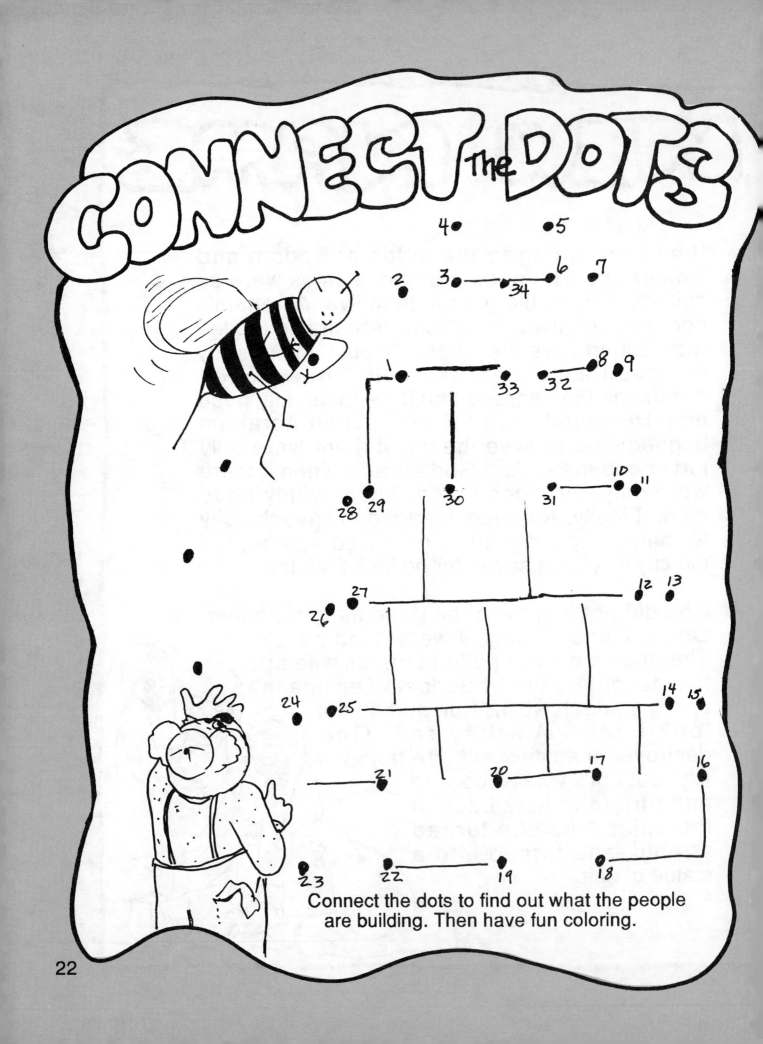

CONNECT the DOTS

Connect the dots to find out what the people are building. Then have fun coloring.

22

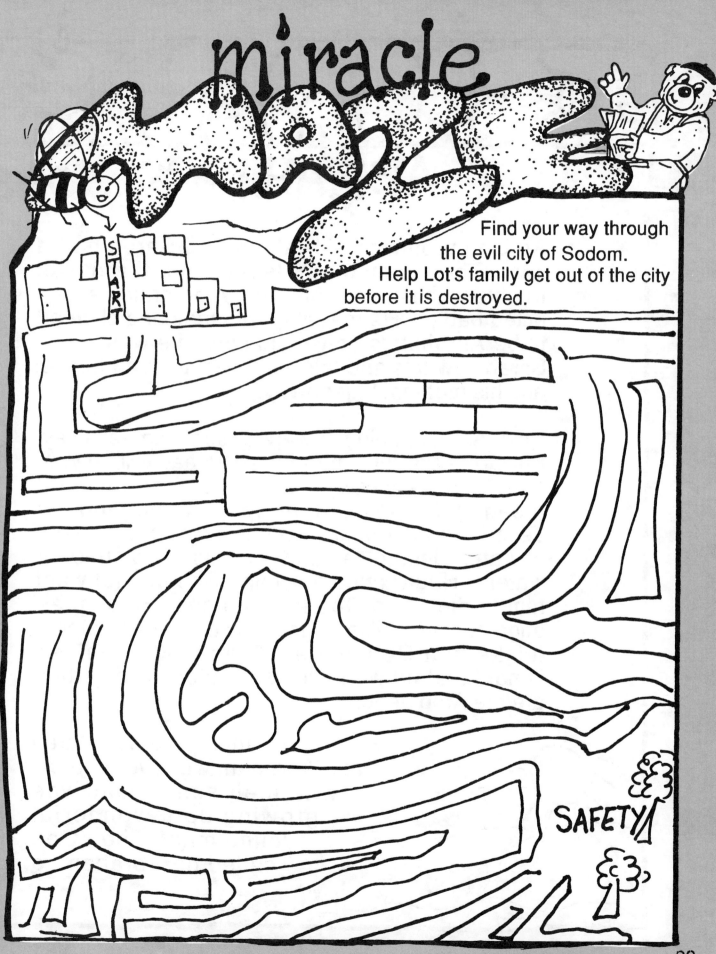

miracle maze

Find your way through the evil city of Sodom. Help Lot's family get out of the city before it is destroyed.

START

SAFETY

ISMAEL
ABRAHAM'S SONS

As God promised, Abraham and Sarah had a son. They named him Isaac. But there was trouble with Ismael. At a party for Isaac, Ismael acted badly. He made fun of Isaac and claimed to be Abraham's only child since he was older. Sarah saw this and told Abraham to send Ismael and his mother Hagar away.

Now, Abraham did not want to send Ismael away. But God said, "Listen to Sarah. Isaac will be your heir." So Abraham gave Hagar and Ismael bread and water for the trip in the hot and dry desert. In the desert, Hagar and Ismael ran out of water. Ismael lay under a bush and cried for water. Hagar cried for help. She did not want him to die. And God heard them. He sent an angel to them. The angel showed Hagar water in a lake that God made. Then God promised Ismael that he would lead a nation. Today they are the Arab people.

Back in Abraham's camp, Sarah and Abraham were very happy with their son. Isaac was growing up a wonderful young man. Then God called on Abraham to

ISAAC

TWO STORIES

prove his faith in Him. "Abraham, give your beloved son as a sacrifice to Me." Howcould he do this? The pagan people who prayed to idols did this, not Abraham. But he had to obey God.

Abraham took Isaac to the mountain. He built an altar. Then Abraham prepared Isaac. Abraham was crying. Suddenly, as Abraham began to give Isaac back to God, an angel stopped him. God did not want Isaac. Not at all. God only wanted to test Abraham's faith. Abraham had proved himself to God.

Looking around, Abraham found a ram to sacrifice. This meant that people never again would offer people, including children, to God.

God blessed Abraham and Isaac. He promised to make them a nation of many. They would have more children than they could count. They would be the nation of Jewish people.

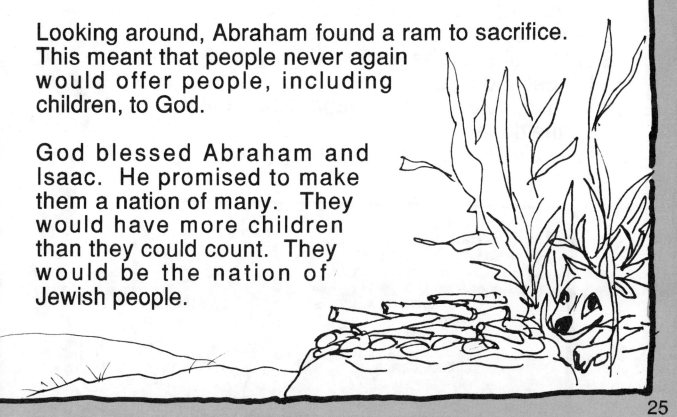

QUESTIONS:

(clues on pages 12,14,16,18,20,21)

1. What did God tell Noah to build?
2. How many of each animal did Noah take on the ark?
3. How many days and nights did it rain?
4. What did God give to man as a promise?
5. What did the people try to build up to the sky?
6. How did God stop them?
7. What was the name of the building and why was it called that?
8. What did Abraham break?
9. What did God promise Abraham?
10. What does Isaac mean?
11. Who lived in the evil city of Sodom?
12. What happened to Lot's wife?
13. Where did Abraham send his first son Ismael and Hagar?
14. What did God send to Hagar and Ismael in the desert?
15. Why did God ask Abraham for Isaac?

ANSWERS:

1) An ark
2) Two (2)
3) Forty (40)
4) A rainbow
5) A tower
6) They were confused
7) Tower of Babel: babbling different languages
8) Idols
9) To make him the father of a great nation.
10) Laughter
11) Abraham's nephew, Lot
12) Turned into a pillar of salt
13) Away into the desert
14) A pond of water
15) To test his faith

26

wordsearch

```
I E L B Y E B O A T W L E R W
D S Y T S U U N A T E U Q B A
M A T E O D M N V S N S E A D
M R M W N L G K H O T E T B Z
A A A M O T S L O D I A T Y R
N H D P I H V P F V Q V R D E
Y S Z A T S L E G N A I E S T
Q Q X B A P R A Y L Z I S U A
Y K N D N K B S P K N O G D W
R B P J L I V E P Z F N O L R
```

Look up and down and find the hidden words
listed below in the letters above.

Find these words in
the letters above.

LOT	STARS	OBEY
NATION	MANY	TEST
IDOLS	TENT	BABY
SARAH	WATER	EVIL
PRAY	ANGELS	

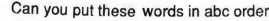

Can you put these words in abc order?

Isaac and

Many years passed. Abraham was old and Sarah had died. It was time for Isaac to marry. He needed a wife from his own family, people who believed in God, not idols. So Abraham called his servant Eliezer. He made Eliezer promise to go back to Abraham's family and find a bride for Isaac. But, the girl would have to live in Canaan with Isaac. Canaan was the land which God promised to them. If she did not want to come to Canaan, Eliezer was freed from his promise to Abraham.

Eliezer took gifts and ten camels. He traveled far to the land of Abraham's brother, Nahor. After awhile, Eliezer stopped and sat down by a well. Young girls were filling their pitchers at this well. How would he know which girl was for Isaac? So he prayed that the right girl would offer water to him and all his camels, when he asked for a drink. Then, a lovely young girl, Rebekah, came to fill her pitcher. When Eliezer asked for a drink she gave him the water. She then offered to water

Rebekah

all his camels. Back and forth she went to the well, giving water to the camels, all ten of them. Camels drink a lot of water. It was a lot of work, but she made sure they all had plenty to drink. "This was the girl for Isaac," thought Eliezer.

Eliezer gave her gifts of bracelets and a ring. He asked about her family and if there was room for him to stay at their home. When he met her father, Eliezer told him that his master, Abraham, had sent him to find a wife for his son, Isaac. Then Eliezer asked Rebekah to return with him to Canaan. Her family asked her if she wanted to go. Rebekah answered, "Yes, I wish to go to Canaan and marry Isaac."

Rebekah left her home with her family's blessings. After a long ride, they arrived in Canaan. Isaac fell in love with Rebekah the minute he saw her. They were married. Later, when Abraham died, the promises that God had made with Abraham were passed on to Isaac.

'I THINK...'

Complete the sentences with your own answers.

1. When I think of Adam and Eve, I _____
_____.

2. If Adam and Eve did not eat the apple, _____
_____.

3. I think that the serpent _____
_____.

4. To me the rainbow is _____
_____.

5. If I were Cain, I would _____
_____.

6. I wish I could see _____
_____.

7. I think that Abraham _____
_____.

8. I think that Lot _____
_____.

9. If I were Rebekah, I _____
_____.

10. When I think of God, I _____
_____.

MAZE

Find your way from the well with water for all ten camels.

WELL START

WATER —END

ESAU & JACOB TWINS

Isaac and Rebekah had twin baby boys. Esau was the first baby born. He was very red and hairy. Jacob was the second born. He was smooth and fair. At birth, Jacob was holding onto the heel of Esau's foot. Isaac favored Esau while Rebekah favored Jacob. Esau, the first-born son had a "birthright" to everything that his father owned. He was a hunter and very gruff. Esau did not care much about his birthright. But Jacob did. Jacob took care of the land and the flocks. He loved God. Esau cared nothing for God.

One day, Esau returned from a hunting trip. He saw Jacob cooking a stew. Now Esau was very hungry and demanded a bowl of the stew. Then Jacob said, "I'll give you this food if you sell me your birthright." Esau didn't care about his birthright, he only wanted the food. And so, Esau gave up his birthright for a bowl of stew.

Years passed and Isaac grew older. It was time to bless his first-born son. He sent Esau hunting. Isaac wanted him to cook his favorite dish. Isaac loved the food that Esau made. So Esau ran to do what his father asked. Meanwhile, Rebekah heard this. She called Jacob and told him what was happening. Rebekah wanted Jacob to get the

JACOB

blessing.   She had a plan. "Jacob, go out and get two goats. I will cook Isaac's favorite dish the way Esau does," said Rebekah.   Since Isaac was nearly blind he could not see Jacob. But he could touch, feel and smell. To trick Isaac, Rebekah had Jacob put on Esau's clothing to smell like him. Then she wrapped furry skins on Jacob's arms and neck. Now he felt like Esau. Next, Jacob went in to his father and said he was Esau.

Did this trick work? Let's see. Isaac asked his son to come near him. Isaac touched him and felt the hands of Esau and smelled the smell of Esau. Yes, Isaac blessed Jacob thinking that it was Esau. But right after Jacob left, Esau came to his father. They knew. Isaac had been tricked and Esau cried to be blessed. Isaac told Esau that his brother was given his blessing. Still, Isaac gave Esau a small blessing. "You will live by your sword and serve your brother. Then you will be free."

This trick made Esau very, very angry. He swore to kill Jacob. Now Jacob had to run for his life. So Rebekah sent him to her brother Laban until Esau's anger passed. To get Isaac's blessing for the trip, Rebekah told Isaac that Jacob was going there to find a wife. Isaac agreed and blessed him.

```
E V X L X U A H C K A I G L D X F V
B A B Y L B B C J C D O I I O E A Y
F H Z K W E R B N Q W T Y R F P T R
O O S P N W S I B Z V O G B W T C L
O L K B Q X S G D C H L V N O Q S O
T B I A W I F E T E K E S I T Y O V
E W N H L J O R A E C F N U I X S E
U G Q L M N P P K R G O I O I C T T
G E T R I C K W F U H O W R K I N E
O W K X Y M M M S B N D T L L E W C
R V N M T T C N I Z N Q K F D H D K
```

Look up and down and find the hidden words
listed below in the letters above.

Find these words in the letters above:

WIFE	GIFTS	FOOD
BRIDE	LOVE	TRICK
TWINS	BABY	SELL
WELL	BOYS	FOOT

Can you put these words in abc order?

34

QUESTIONS

(Clues on Pages 24,25,28,29,32,33)

1. What did Abraham and Isaac sacrifice on the mountain?
2. Whom did Abraham send to find a wife for Isaac?
3. Why did she have to come to live in Canaan?
4. How did Eliezer choose a girl?
5. How many camels did Eliezer have?
6. Who was the first-born of Rebekah's twins?
7. What was Jacob holding on to when he was born?
8. What did the first-born get?
9. What did Esau sell to Jacob?
10. What did Jacob buy the birthright with?
11. How did Jacob get Isaac's blessing instead of Esau?
12. Why was Jacob able to trick Isaac?
13. Who helped Jacob?
14. Where did Jacob go?
15. Why did Isaac give Jacob his blessing when he left?

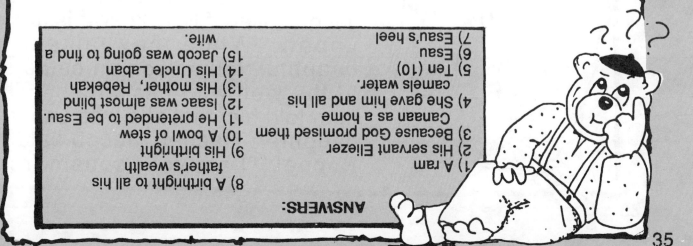

ANSWERS:

1) A ram
2) His servant Eliezer
3) Because God promised them Canaan as a home
4) She gave him and all his camels water.
5) Ten (10)
6) Esau
7) Esau's heel
8) A birthright to all his father's wealth
9) His birthright
10) A bowl of stew
11) He pretended to be Esau.
12) Isaac was almost blind
13) His mother, Rebekah
14) His Uncle Laban
15) Jacob was going to find a wife.

Jacob ♡ ♡

Jacob was running away from his brother Esau. He would go to his uncle Laban, where they did not worship idols. Maybe he would find a wife there. So Jacob traveled all day. Now he was tired and needed to rest. So he lay down on the ground, using a rock for a pillow. In his sleep he dreamt that he saw a ladder. It started on the ground and reached all the way up to Heaven. Angels of God were walking up and down the ladder.

Then the Lord God spoke to Jacob: "I am the Lord, I will give you and your children this land. Through your children the families of the earth will be blessed. I am with you and will be with you wherever you are. I will return you to this land and not leave you until I have done what I say."

Jacob awoke from his dream. He marked the spot with the rock he had used as a pillow. He called this place Beth-El, meaning "House of God." Then he traveled on. He came upon shepherds near a well. Jacob asked if they knew his uncle, Laban. While they talked, a beautiful young woman came up to the well with her sheep. The men told him that she was Laban's daughter, Rachel. Jacob said to Rachel: "I am your cousin from

♥ Rachel

Canaan." Then she ran to tell her father, who welcomed Jacob into his home.

Jacob fell in love with Rachel. He told Laban he would work seven years to marry her. Jacob loved Rachel so much that the seven years went by very quickly. At the wedding, the bride wore a heavy veil. Then Jacob found he had married Rachel's sister, Leah. Angry, Jacob demanded: "Why did you trick me like this? I love Rachel!" Laban said that his older daughter had to marry first. But Jacob could marry Rachel, also. Of course he must work seven more years. Well, Jacob married Rachel and worked seven more years for Laban. Then he worked another six years to pay Laban for cattle. Finally, after twenty years, Jacob and his family left to go home to Canaan.

Now Jacob did not know if his brother Esau had forgiven him for stealing his birthright and blessing. Jacob was afraid to see Esau. One night, on the way home, an angel of the Lord fought with Jacob . Afterward, the angel told Jacob that his name would be Israel. This means Prince of God, because he had struggled with both man and God and survived. The next morning, when Esau saw Jacob, Esau ran up to him and hugged him. They both cried. All was forgiven. Jacob and his family had come home to the land of Canaan, as God had promised.

Help Jacob find his way from his home in Canaan, with his parents Isaac and Rebekah, to Haran, where his Uncle Laban lives.

CROSSWORD PUZZLE

(Clues on pages 18-19, 24-25, 28-29, 32-33, 36-37)

Use the questions below to fill in the answers to the puzzle. Have fun.

Across:

3. "Kid"   7. Rest

8. False stone gods

10. ☆ ☆

12. ooooo + ooooo

13. (shirt drawing)

Down:

1. (arm/muscle drawing)   2. (rock drawing)

4. Two alike   5. (basket drawing)

6. (corn drawing)   7. 2 + 5 =

9. (salt shaker drawing)   11. (tent drawing)

WORD LIST

ROCK
GOAT
CORN
TWINS
SLEEP
HEEL
WELL
TEN
SEVEN
SALT
IDOLS
STARS
COAT
TENT

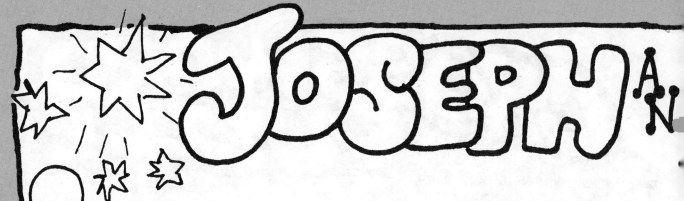

JOSEPH AN

Jacob was now called Israel. He had twelve sons. They would be the twelve tribes of Israel. Joseph, his favorite son, was a dreamer. Jacob made him a beautiful coat of many colors. His brothers did not like that, or his dreams.

In one dream they were all gathering sheaves, or bundles of grain, and his bundle stood up straight while all of theirs bowed down to his. In another dream, he saw the sun, moon and eleven stars bow down to him. Even Jacob said it wasn't nice to say that his father, mother and brothers would bow to him.

One day, Jacob's sons were out in the fields feeding the flocks. He sent Joseph to see how they were doing. When his brothers saw him they wanted to kill him, but the oldest stopped them. Instead, they took his coat and threw him into a pit. Now they planned to sell him. But while they took a break to eat, some men found Joseph in the pit. These men pulled him out and sold him to a caravan. When his brothers returned to the pit, it was empty. They thought that Joseph had been killed by a wild animal. They put animal blood on

THE DREAMS

Joseph's coat. Then they took the coat to Jacob to show that Joseph was killed. Jacob mourned his son for a long time.

But Joseph was not dead. He was taken to Egypt and sold as a slave to an Egyptian. But the Egyptian got angry at him and put Joseph in jail. Still, God was with Joseph. He was put incharge of other prisoners. Pharaoh's baker and butler were also in jail. They told him about their dreams. Joseph understood dreams. He said that the baker would die and the butler would return to work for Pharaoh. And it all came true.

Later, Pharaoh had a dream. He saw seven fat cows eating grass. Then seven skinny cows came out of the river and ate the seven fat cows. Pharaoh had another dream. There were seven ears of good corn. Then seven dried up ears of corn grew and ate up the good corn. All the wise men could not explain it. Then the butler remembered Joseph in jail. And Pharaoh sent for Joseph.

Joseph said God was showing them what was going to happen. The two dreams were one. First there would be seven years of food, then seven years of hunger. Joseph told them to put away grain from the good years for the hungry years. Pharaoh was pleased. He put Joseph in charge, over all of Egypt, just as Joseph had dreamed.

What is it?

Color the different areas to find a full picture. Use the guide below. What do you see in the picture?

R - Red   Y - Yellow   G - Green

B - Brown   O - Orange

42

wordsearch

```
R L B P V V U Z Q W P L H V K N R R
S E H I O Y N W N H O W I F D S X A
A O V S H E C B V Z R X A P R H K F
E T N I M N L H M I F V G L E T Y R
Q D Y S R P E C I S R A E L A L C E
X R I D R O L O L Q W Q C P M J N S
R B Q B I C V A N R O C I O V V E T
J O H K L I L T P L B V D F W A V J
M V C W E L L L N I G D J A R S E W
Q J B K L P M H V O H X G Q V B S R
U P Q T X L R O L O C R W H S Y I K
```

Find these words in the letters above.

COWS	WELL
LORD	ISRAEL	DREAM
UNCLE	SONS	CORN
ROCK	COAT	RIVER
SEVEN	COLOR	REST

Can you put these words in abc order?

Israel

Joseph was governor of Egypt. He was almost as important as Pharaoh. There were seven good years and then seven dry years. There was no rain, no water, and the land dried up. People had no food. But Egypt had food that was stored away.

Jacob sent his sons to Egypt to buy food. His youngest son, Benjamin, stayed with him. When they arrived, Joseph knew who they were. But they did not know him. He asked them about themselves and their family. They told him that they were sons of Israel. The youngest, Benjamin, was with their father. Another brother, Joseph, was dead. Pretending that they were spies, Joseph had them arrested. He told them that he would keep one brother in Egypt and send the others home. He would know they were not spies if they brought back their youngest brother.

Jacob's sons traveled home. They told their father all about being called spies. They said that the governor kept one brother,

in Egypt

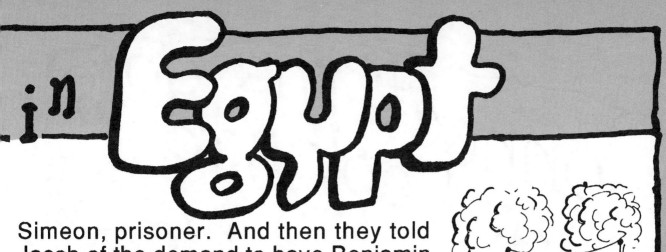

Simeon, prisoner. And then they told Jacob of the demand to have Benjamin brought to Egypt. Reuben, who was the oldest, said that he would be responsible for Benjamin's safety. So Benjamin went to Egypt with the others.

They returned to Egypt with gifts. They brought their brother, Benjamin, to Joseph. Joseph treated them to dinner. He said now he knew they were honest. Then Joseph secretly had his helper place his gold wine goblet in Benjamin's bag of grain. After they left, Joseph had his guards chase after them and search their bags. They found the wine goblet in Benjamin's bag. Then Joseph said that Benjamin must stay as his slave. All the rest could return home. Reuben begged Joseph to take him instead. Now, Joseph saw his brothers' love and cried. He told them that he was their brother, Joseph. He sent them to bring his father, Jacob, to Egypt.

Jacob was very happy to see his son, Joseph, alive and well. Pharaoh welcomed Jacob, his sons and family to live out the dry years in Egypt. And that is how Israel came to live in Egypt-land.

Connect the dots and color, too

Connect the dots to find out what the names of all the tribes are on. Then have fun coloring.

Next, take a blank paper and draw your own family tree.

MORE TRIVIA

QUESTIONS:

(Clues on pages 36-37, 40-41, 44-45)

1. Where did Jacob go when he left home?
2. When Jacob stopped to rest, what did he use for a pillow?
3. What did Jacob see in his dream?
4. Where did Jacob first meet Rachel?
5. What did Jacob argree to do for Laban, in order to marry Rachel?
6. What happened at the wedding and how did he get to marry Rachel?
7. What happened between Easu and Jacob when they met?
8. What was Jacob's new name and how did he get it? How many sons did Jacob have? What were they called?
10. What did Jacob make for his son Joseph?
11. What was special about Joseph?
12. How did Joseph get to Egypt?
13. How did Joseph help Pharaoh and what happened to Joseph?
14. What happened when the brothers went to Egypt for food?
15. What did Jacob have put in Benjamin's bag?

ANSWERS:

1) His uncle Laban
2) A rock
3) A ladder with angels, God spoke to him.
4) By a well
5) Work seven years
6) A switch–he was married to Rachel's older sister, Leah, Jacob promised to work another seven years if he also married Rachel
7) They hugged and all was forgiven
8) Israel he struggled with an angel, and God gave him the name
9) Twelve (12) The twelve tribes of Israel
10) A coat of many colors
11) He was a dreamer
12) He was sold to a traveling caravan
13) He interpreted his dreams
14) Joseph said they were spies–He kept Simeon in jail until they brought Benjamin to Egypt
15) A gold wine cup

47

MOSES

The new Pharaoh was selfish and very mean. The Egyptians were jealous of the Israelites, who had power and money. Hebrew families filled the land. The Egyptians were afraid that they would take over Egypt. So Pharaoh made the Israelites slaves.

Pharaoh feared that the Israelites might fight against Egypt. He ordered all newborn baby boys killed so there would be no strong Israelite men left. One mother hid her baby. She made a waterproof basket and put him into it. Her daughter, Miriam, took the baby in the basket to the river. She put it into the water. Then Miriam hid in the bushes to watch the basket.

Along came Pharaoh's daughter to bathe in the river. As the princess entered the water, she saw a basket. She told her servant to get it. The princess looked inside. It was a baby! She decided to keep it. Now she needed a nurse. Miriam went over to the princess and said, "I know of a Hebrew woman who could nurse

...IS BORN

the baby." (Secretly, the baby's mother.)

The princess called him "Moses" which means, "taken from the water." His mother was his nurse. Moses grew up with his people, learning all their ways. Then it came time for Moses to live in Pharaoh's palace. There he learned all that a prince would learn. One day, when he was grown up, he saw a slave being beaten by an Egyptian master. He had to save the Hebrew slave. Moses fought with the Egyptian and killed him. Now Pharaoh could have Moses killed. So Moses had to run far away.

Years passed and the king of Egypt had died. A new ruler became Pharaoh. But the Israelites' lives did not get any better. They cried to God to save them and God heard them.

Meanwhile, far away, Moses worked as a shepherd. One day, he saw a bush on fire. The bush was not burning, but there was a fire. God called out to Moses: "I am the God of your father, God of Abraham, Isaac and Jacob." God told him that he had heard the cries of his people in Egypt. He was sending Moses to free the Israelites from slavery. He would lead them to the promised land of Canaan. Moses took his wife and son to Egypt. With God's help, he was going to tell Pharaoh: "Let my people go!"

```
G O O D D I L J N E Y W V F Y C Z E
F P J H E A J F G K V E J G T N K R
E M O S E S E F I N D A A L I Y Q X
E B X M E A N L F R P L L R P G P T
R B P V V Q H S U B E A X S S I S V
F W A B T S U W I N E N A U R S A B
I B I G Z R Y B D Q H D B H E P J J
H J Y E M J I K Q R V W R Q V I J X
H C N W X K Y N T T U X C O I E N S
N J W Y N K Z S G Q A P B R R S L X
```

Look up and down for the words.
Have a good time searching.

Find these words in the letters above:

BUSH   BAG   GOOD
FIRE   LAND   YEARS
FREE   MEAN   SPIES
MOSES   SLAVE   WINE
LEAD   RIVER

50   Can you put these words in abc order?

Connect the dots to find out
what the princess has found.
Then have fun coloring.

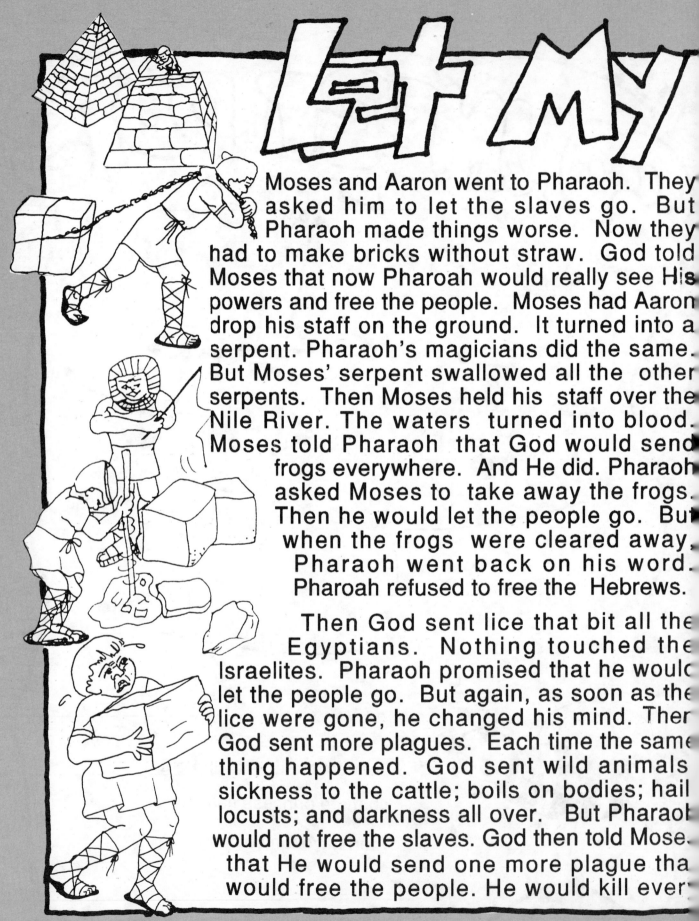

Let My

Moses and Aaron went to Pharaoh. They asked him to let the slaves go. But Pharaoh made things worse. Now they had to make bricks without straw. God told Moses that now Pharoah would really see His powers and free the people. Moses had Aaron drop his staff on the ground. It turned into a serpent. Pharaoh's magicians did the same. But Moses' serpent swallowed all the other serpents. Then Moses held his staff over the Nile River. The waters turned into blood. Moses told Pharaoh that God would send frogs everywhere. And He did. Pharaoh asked Moses to take away the frogs. Then he would let the people go. But when the frogs were cleared away, Pharaoh went back on his word. Pharoah refused to free the Hebrews.

Then God sent lice that bit all the Egyptians. Nothing touched the Israelites. Pharaoh promised that he would let the people go. But again, as soon as the lice were gone, he changed his mind. Then God sent more plagues. Each time the same thing happened. God sent wild animals; sickness to the cattle; boils on bodies; hail; locusts; and darkness all over. But Pharaoh would not free the slaves. God then told Moses that He would send one more plague that would free the people. He would kill every

PEOPLE GO!

first-born Egyptian.

The Israelites were told to paint the doorposts of their homes with lamb's blood. God would see this mark and pass over their homes in the night, when He would kill the Egyptian first-born. That night they ate roast lamb and unleavened bread. They had no time to let the bread rise. The angel of death came and passed over the marked homes. The first-born in every Egyptian house died, even Pharaoh's son. Pharaoh cried to Moses to take the people and leave.

Moses led the people into the desert. They stoppped at the Sea of Reeds. Pharaoh sent his army after them. Then Moses stretched his staff over the waters and they opened up. The Israelites walked across on dry land. The army followed. Again, Moses lifted his staff over the waters. The sea closed up, drowning all the Egyptians. Now the Israelites were free.

What Do You Think...

Complete the sentences with your own answers.

1. Being a twin would be _____

_____.

2. When I think of Jacob and Esau, I _____

_____.

3. I think that when Esau sold his birthright, _____

_____.

4. Tricking Isaac for the blessing was _____

_____.

5. I think that Jacob's dream _____

_____.

6. If I were Jacob at the wedding, I _____

_____.

7. I think Joseph's brothers _____

_____ _____.

8. When the brothers came to Egypt, I think that Joseph

_____.

9. I think that when Israel was in Egypt-land, ___

_____.

10. I have had dreams about _____

_____

_____.

TRIVIA

QUESTIONS
(Clues on pages 48-49, 50-52)

1. In what did Miriam carry her baby brother?
2. Who found the basket?
3. What did she call the baby?
4. Who took care of Moses as a baby?
5. Why did Moses have to run away from Egypt?
6. What did Moses work at?
7. What did Moses see burning, and what happened?
8. What did God tell Moses to do?
9. What did Moses' staff turn into?
10. Who was Aaron?
11. Name two of the ten plagues.
12. What did the Israelites do so that the angel of death would pass over their homes?
13. The people ran until they came to the Sea of _____?
14. How did the people cross the Sea of Reeds?
15. What happened to Pharaoh's army?

ANSWERS:

1) A waterproofed basket
2) Pharaoh's daughter, the princess
3) Moses
4) His mother
5) He killed an Egyptian
6) Shepherding
7) A bush, but it did not burn. God spoke to him.
8) Free the Israelites from slavery and lead them to Canaan
9) A serpent
10) Moses' older brother
11) Blood-Frogs-Lice-wild beasts-sickness of animals-boils-hail-locusts-darkness-death of firstborn.
13) Reeds
14) God separated the waters and they walked on dry land.
15) They drowned when the sea closed up

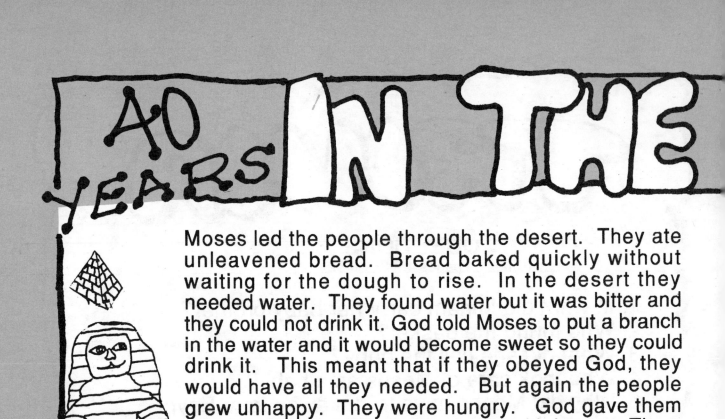

Moses led the people through the desert. They ate unleavened bread. Bread baked quickly without waiting for the dough to rise. In the desert they needed water. They found water but it was bitter and they could not drink it. God told Moses to put a branch in the water and it would become sweet so they could drink it. This meant that if they obeyed God, they would have all they needed. But again the people grew unhappy. They were hungry. God gave them manna. It tasted like wafers made with honey. There was always enough for everyone, every day. On the sixth day they had to collect enough for two days. They were to rest on the seventh day, the Sabbath.

The Israelites met many enemies on their journey. It took forty years to reach Caanan, because the people sinned. Moses took the people to Mount Sinai where he went up the mountain to talk with God. God gave Moses Ten Commandments to bring to the people:

1) I am the Lord, thy God you shall have no other gods.

2) You shall not make or bow down to any statues of gods.

3) You shall not take God's name in vain.

4) Remember the Sabbath and keep it holy.

DESERT

5) Honor your father and your mother.
6) You shall not kill.
7) You shall not commit adultery.
8) You shall not steal.
9) You shall not lie about others.
10) You shall not want to take things that belong to others.

Moses went up to God. He was there forty days and forty nights. While he was gone the people became scared. They went to Aaron and demanded that he make a god since Moses was not there. Aaron used their gold to made a golden calf. The people worshipped it. They were singing and dancing around the idol in a most terrible way. God heard this and was going to kill the people. Moses begged God not to kill them. But then Moses saw the golden calf. He was so angry that he smashed the holy tablets.

Moses went back up the mountain to ask God's forgiveness. God wrote two new tablets. After nearly 40 years in the desert all the people who had left Egypt and sinned were dead. Now new people of Israel were to enter Caanan. Moses chose Joshua to be the new leader. Moses could not go into the promised land. He went up Mount Nebo in Moab. He saw Canaan from the mountain top. Moses died there and was buried on the mountain.

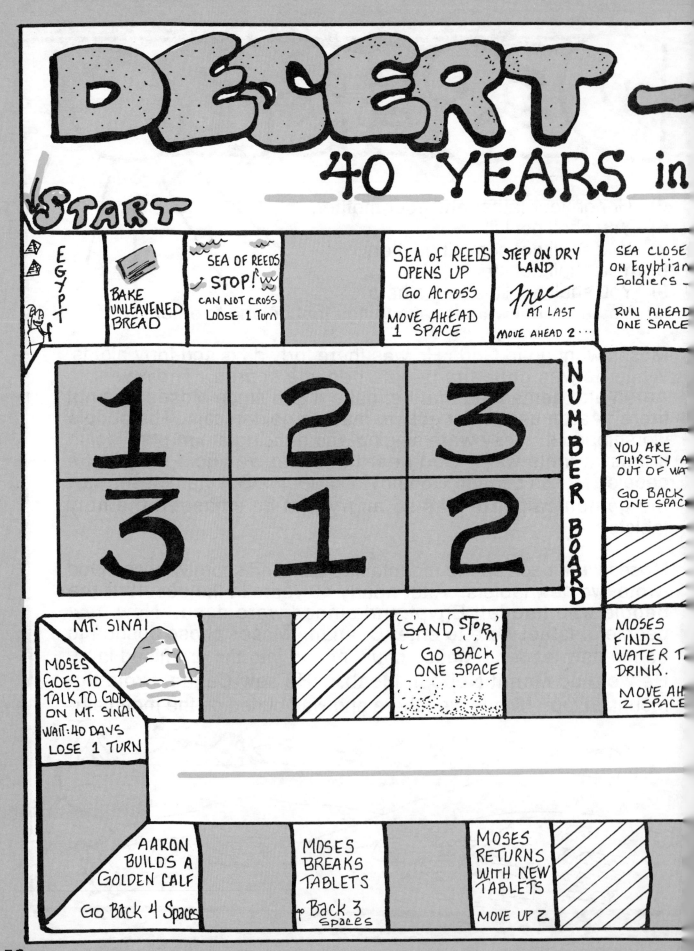

BOARD GAME
the DESERT

CAMELS ARE GETTING TIRED. GO BACK ONE SPACE	A GOOD DAY TO TRAVEL TAKE ANOTHER — TURN —	TIME FOR A NAP IN YOUR TENT. SKIP ONE TURN

* Use coins or buttons as markers. You can even design your own Bible characters of cardboard cutouts.

* Use the number square below to find out how many spaces to move. Cover your eyes and point to a number if you land on a line, add up the two boxes. Or use a coin to drop on the box.

* Move the marker along the board and follow the instructions written in the box on which you land.

* One move to a turn

* The first person to get to Canaan wins.

CANAAN

MOSES CHOOSES JOSHUA AS THE NEW LEADER

TIME TO TRAVEL GO FORWARD 3 SPACES

GOING THE WRONG WAY GO BACK 1 SPACE

YOU WON The Battle GO FORWARD 3 SPACES

SEND SPIES TO SEE THE NEW LAND WAIT AND SKIP 1 TURN

SPIES RETURN MOVE FORWARD 2 SPACES

MOSES GOES UP MT. NEBO SAY GOODBYE AND GO BACK 3 SPACES

Feet are wet. Go back 5 SPACES WALK ACROSS THE JORDAN RIVER

SAND IN YOUR EYE MOVE 2 SPACES BACK ←

THE SUN IS VERY HOT — FIND SHADE GO BACK ONE SPACE

LOOK OUT - SPIES ARE AHEAD - ENEMIES GO BACK ONE SPACE

STOP TO FIGHT THE ENEMY SKIP 1 TURN

JOSHUA Leads the people

Moses could not go into Caanan. So he chose his helper Joshua to lead the people. First Joshua sent men to check out the land. Then it was time for the Israelites to cross the Jordan. After 40 years they were in Canaan. It was the eve of the Passover feast.

The people of Jericho were afraid. They locked the gates to the city. God told Joshua how to enter the city. Once a day for six days the people walked around the walls of the city. Then the priests blew the trumpets. On the seventh day they walked around seven times. Then they shouted, making lots of noise. The walls of Jericho came tumbling down. The Israelites entered the city.

Next, Joshua told the men to attack the city of Ai. But when they reached the gate they were to turn around and walk away. The men of Ai would open the gates and run out after them. Israelites woud hide by the gate. Then they would sneak in from behind and enter the city. So they took the city by trickery. There were more wars ahead. With God's help, Joshua led them through six years of battles.

Joshua divided the land. All the tribes were given land, except the Levites. The Levites are the people whom God selected to serve Him. The others gave the Levites homes, food and clothing. Many people wanted to honor Joshua. Each tribe gave him a piece of their land. He made six safe cities. There, an innocent person could go to be safe.

Joshua told the leaders that because they had obeyed God's rules, they won and did well. He warned them that they must obey God. Later, Joshua died and new leaders were chosen. As the people stopped obeying God, God took away His help, just as Joshua had warned them He would.

62 Help Joshua cross the Jordon River and enter into the city of Jericho.

CROSSWORD puzzle....

(Clues on pages 40-41, 44-45, 48-49, 52-53, 56-57, 60-61)

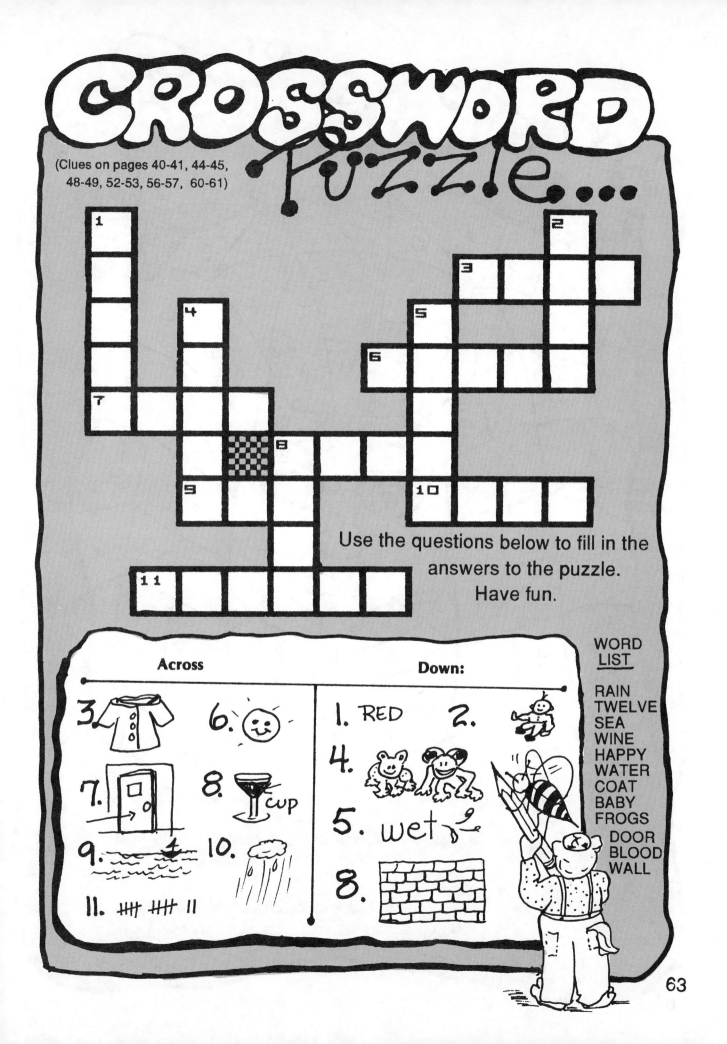

Use the questions below to fill in the answers to the puzzle.
Have fun.

Across

3. 6.

7. 8. cup

9. 10.

11. ||||| ||||| ||

Down:

1. RED 2.

4.

5. wet

8.

WORD LIST

RAIN
TWELVE
SEA
WINE
HAPPY
WATER
COAT
BABY
FROGS
DOOR
BLOOD
WALL

63

What is it?

Color the different areas to find a full picture. Use the guide below. What do you see?

R - Red   G - Green   B - Brown
Y - Yellow   O - Orange

Connect the Dots

Connect the dots to find out what is important to follow. Then have fun coloring.

SAMSON'S

Samson was a leader of great strength. He never cut his hair. Samson found out that he was very strong when he met a lion and killed it with his bare hands. A year later, he saw the dead lion's skeleton with bees and honey on it. He made a riddle about the lion and honey. When he got married he made a bet with 30 Philistine men. If they could solve his riddle he would give them all new robes. But if they lost, they would give him 30 robes. The riddle: "Out of the eater came food; out of the strong came sweetness." No one could solve it.

The men threatened Samson's bride. She had to get the answer for them. So she cried to Samson until he told her. Then she told the men. Then the men told Samson: "A lion is strong and honey is sweet." Samson was angry. He attacked another town and took 30 robes to pay the bet. Then he burned the Philistines' fields. His people were afraid of the Philistines. So they tied up Samson and took him to the Philistines. Samson broke the ropes holding him. Then he killed 1000 Philistines with the jawbone of an ass. Israel was freed.

Samson ruled Israel for 20 years. Then he fell in love with a beautiful woman, Delilah. She was a spy for the Philistines. She begged him to tell her the secret of his strength. He told her that if he was tied up in wet vines he would become weak. She tied him up. But he broke the

STRENGTH

vines. Then he told her it had to be new ropes. The same thing happened. Then he told her that if she tied his hair he would become weak. Then she tied his hair and called the spies. But he broke away. Now Delilah was angry. He finally told her the truth. He never cut his hair as a promise to God. If he cut his hair he would lose his strength. That night she had the Philistines cut his hair. This time he was too weak to fight. The Philistines blinded him and put him into jail.

In prison, his hair grew and his strength returned. Samson was taken to a big party with the king.

Thousands of people were there. He asked a boy for help putting his hands on the pillars. He asked God for help and strength one more time. Then, standing between two pillars, Samson pulled with all his might. The roof came crashing down. So Samson killed all the Philistines and himself, too.

Hidden Pictures

How many frogs can you find?

```
Q S D M F B V H D O V E H R P O V L L
I S X N O O D E R B F A E H A I R U S
S A C N Z I Q M A N N A W R K I M R T
P P T O X L K A E S S M H A F P U Y R
B Y E H Q S A U O D A L A A L N R U O
L G B E T I G K Q Z R M N O B L T I N
O A D S C A H X B B D O W H L H Q S G
O X L H W T E R H A I L W I H D Q M Q
D C E C F E F D C F Y Z X N W P V Z G
T F H M K N F R O G S Z P I D D R E P
V N T J U L A N X L V P B G E D L E H
```

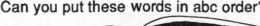

See how many of these words you can find.

TEN
DEATH
PASS
SEA
DROWN

MANNA
WALL
STRONG
HAIR

HAIL
BLOOD
FROGS
FREE
BOILS

Can you put these words in abc order?

Which one is Different..

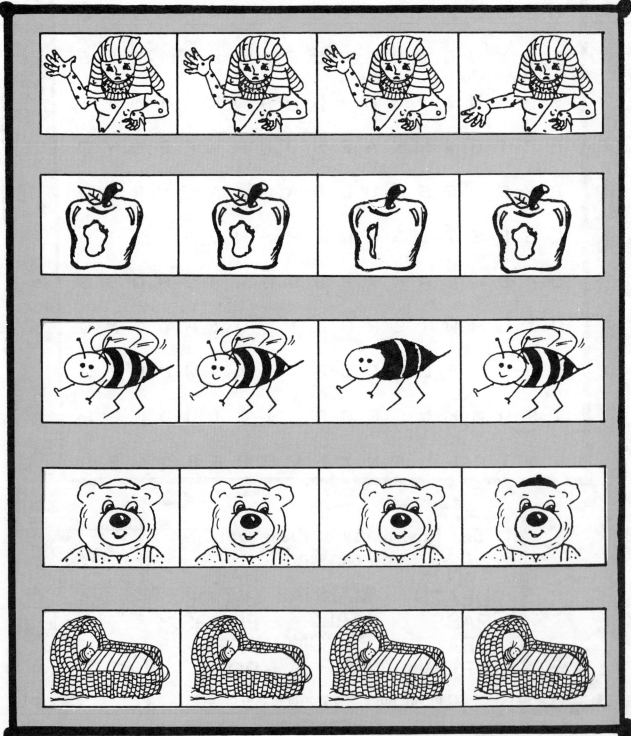

70 Circle the picture in each row that looks different from the other three pictures. Now color them all for fun.

RUTH'S Story

Naomi was a widow in a strange land. She had two daughters-in law, Orpah and Ruth. They were also widows. They had no children. Naomi decided that it was time to go back to her own land. She wanted Orpah and Ruth to go back to their families. There they could remarry and have children. But they loved her very much and did not want to leave her.

Naomi said they would be strangers in her land. Orpah obeyed Naomi. With tears she went back to her family. But Ruth refused to leave Naomi. She said to her mother-in-law: "Wherever you go, I will go. Your home will be my home. Your people will be my people and your God will be my God."

Together, Ruth and Naomi went to Judah. For food, Ruth gathered grain that fell in the fields. This was called gleaning. Ruth gleaned in the fields belonging to a man called Boaz. Boaz saw Ruth in the field. He liked her. Boaz told his men to drop extra grain for her to collect. Boaz asked Ruth to become his wife. They were married and had a son named Obed. Ruth was the great-grandmother of Israel's King David.

(Color the picture of Ruth, Orpah and Naomi)

Samuel

Hannah was a childless Hebrew woman. She prayed to God for a child. After awhile, she was blessed with a son. She called him Samuel. Samuel means "asked of God." When Samuel was old enough, she brought him to Eli, the temple priest. Samuel would live with him and learn to serve God. Samuel was a very good child. One night Samuel heard his name called. He went to Eli. But Eli had not called him. Eli told Samuel that it was the Lord calling. If he heard the voice again he was to tell God he was listening. Samuel went back to bed. He heard his name called again. This time he answered. God spoke to him. God said that Eli's sons were bad. Samuel would become the next high priest.

The Philistines attacked Israel. The Israelities lost. Eli's sons were priests. They carried the Holy Ark from the great temple to the Israelite camp. The Philistiines saw this. They were afraid the ark would give Israel strength. So they attacked the camp and killed the priests. Then they took the ark.

King Saul

When Eli heard that his sons were dead and the ark was stolen, he died. The Philistines took the Holy Ark to the temple of their god. Bad things happened to them. The people became sick and died. So the Philistines gave the Holy Ark back to the Israel. They hoped that would make the bad things stop. Samuel told the Israelites: "If you serve God, you will be safe." And Israel had peace.

After many years the people wanted a king. Samuel tried to tell them that a king would not be good. But God told Samuel to listen to the people. God would help Samuel choose a king for Israel. At that time, a young man named Saul came to find Samuel. He needed help finding his father's lost donkeys. Samuel saw Saul and knew that God had chosen him. Samuel presented him to the people as the king of Israel. That day God sent a sign of rain and thunder.

Israel won many wars with King Saul. But Saul became boastful and selfish. He disobeyed God's commands. Samuel told Saul that God now rejected him as king. Samuel never saw Saul again. Saul still ruled Israel for many years. He died on his own sword in battle.

DONKEY SEARCH MAZE

IN

Follow Saul on his search for his father's donkeys until he finds the priest Samuel.

OUT

CONNECT the DOTS

Connect the dots to find out what Saul would get to wear. Then have fun coloring.

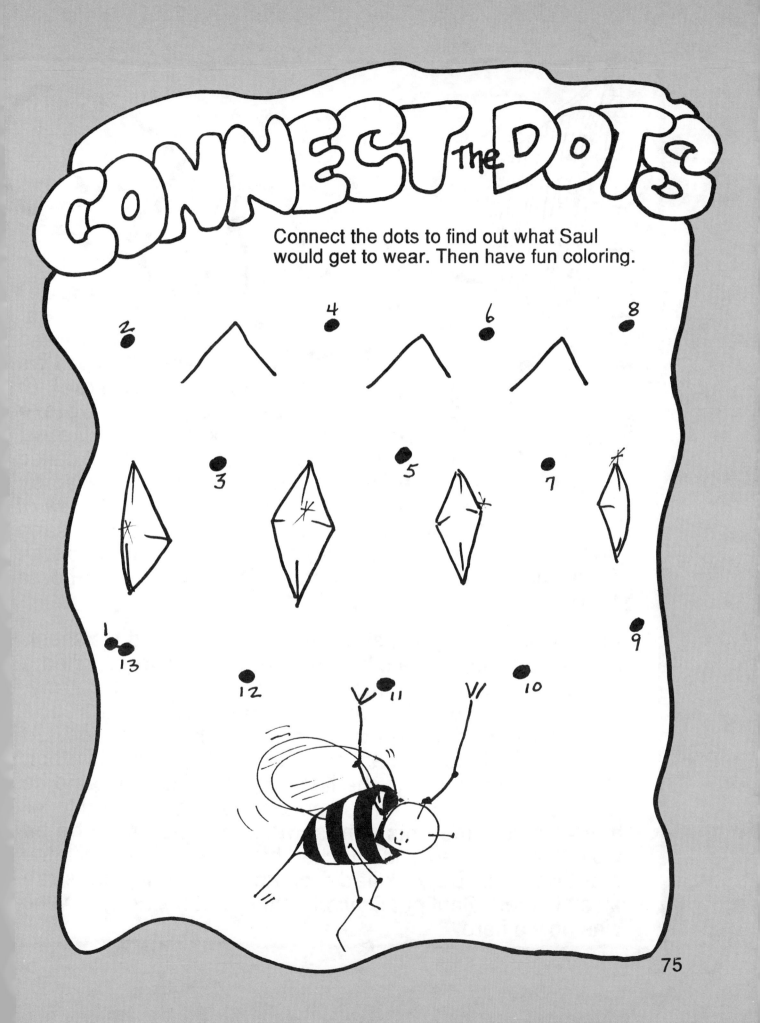

DAVID

Samuel chose a young shepherd boy named David as the future king of Israel. It would be many years before David became king. So David returned to tend his sheep until God called him. Meanwhile, King Saul was bothered by what he called evil spirits. Saul's servants knew of David, the shepherd boy who played the harp and sang songs. So they sent for David to play and help soothe Saul's pain. King Saul felt better. David went back home to his sheep.

David was a very good shepherd. He had saved his sheep from a lion with just a slingshot. Another time he killed a bear. But David was too young to fight with the army. Three of his brothers were fighting the Philistines. His father was worried. He told David to take them food. At the battlefield, he saw Goliath, the giant Philistine warrior. David told about killing the lion and the bear. He said he wanted to fight the giant. Then the giant threatened to kill him. David aimed his slingshot. With one stone he hit Goliath in the head and knocked him down. Then with the giant's sword, David killed Goliath. The Philistiines ran away in fear. Saul put David in charge of his army. David was now a hero.

The Shepherd King

Saul asked David to live with him and his son, Jonathan. David and Jonathan became as close as brothers. But Saul was jealous of David. So Saul sent him to war. He hoped that David would be killed. But David returned. Then Saul told Jonathan that he wanted David killed. A true friend, Jonathan warned David: "Run away and save yourself!"

Later, King Saul and Jonathan died in a battle against the Philistines. Saul threw himself on his own sword. He did not want to be taken captive. David became king of Israel. David had promised to care for Jonathan's son Mephibosheth. David found him alive, but crippled. Then David brought him to live with him.

King David conquered Jerusalem. He made it the center of Israel. He brought the Holy Ark to Jerusalem. Then David wanted to build a beautiful temple. But God told him not to build it. The temple would be built by David's son when he became king. God wanted the temple built by men of peace. David was king of Israel for 40 years.

Color Puzzle

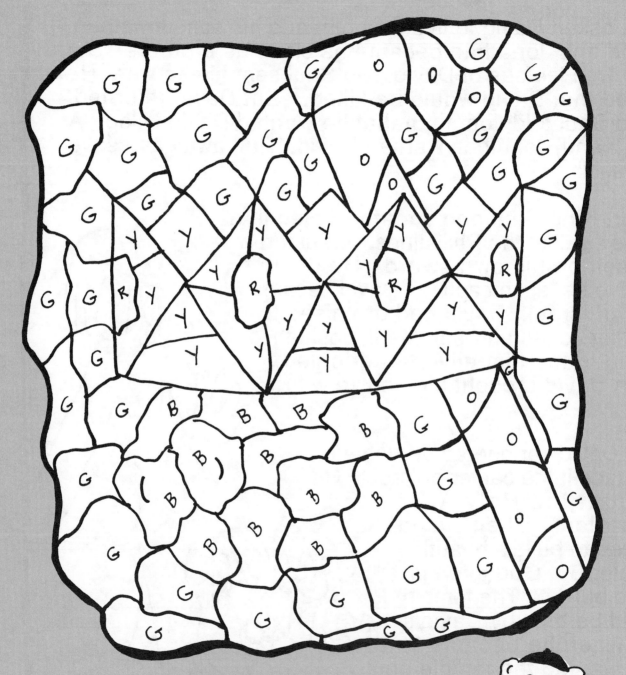

Color the different areas to find a full picture.
Use the guide below. What do you see in the picture?

Red - R   Yellow - Y   Green - G   Brown - B   Orange - O

MATCHING

WORDS AND PICTURES

WORKER

BASKET   DRAG

EGYPTIAN

BABY   SLAVE

PYRAMID

APPLE   KING

PHARAOH

BRICKS   CRY

Draw a line to the right name that goes with each of the pictures. Then have fun coloring.

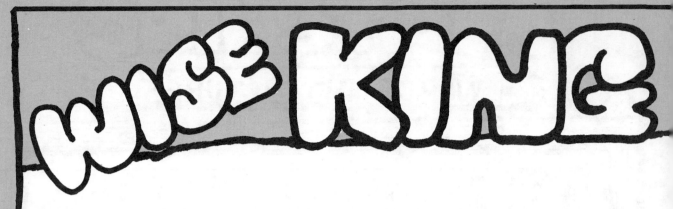

WISE KING

King David chose his son, Solomon, to be the next king. When David was dying, his oldest son tried to become king. David told the high priest to anoint Solomon as king right away. One night, Solomon dreamed that God spoke to him. God offered him whatever he needed. Solomon asked for wisdom. God gave him a wise and understanding heart. If he obeyed God's laws he would have a long, rich life.

Once, two women came to see the king. The women lived in the same house. They had babies at the same time. One woman said that theother woman's baby had died. Then, during the night, she switched babies. She left her dead baby and took the live baby. Solomon listened to both of them. Then he called for his sword. He said that he would cut the child in half. Then each woman would have half a baby. One woman said nothing. The other woman called out to save the child. "Give it to the other woman," she cried. She would give up the child to save its life. Indeed, she was the real mother.

SOLOMON

Solomon built a temple to God. It took fifteen years to build. The temple was beautiful, with gold and jewels. Now, the Holy Ark had a home. Solomon dedicated the temple. He built himself homes. He built cities and ships. The Queen of Sheba heard of the wise and rich Solomon. She traveled to see him for herself. What she saw was more wonderful than she ever imagined. She asked King Solomon many questions. King Solomon gave her very wise answers.

Later, Solomon turned to other gods. This made God very angry. God punished Solomon by dividing the kingdom after Solomon died. Solomon's son, Rehoboam, became king. But another king, Jeroboam, ruled all the tribes of Israel except for Judah.

In honor of King David's love and service, God let King Rehoboam, David's grandson, rule over the tribe of Judah.

Fun Crossword Puzzle

(Clues on pages 66-67, 70-71, 72-73, 76-77, 80-81)

Use the questions below to fill in the answers to the puzzle. Have fun.

WORD LIST

SWORD
STONE
GIANT
BABY
LOVE
STRONG
LION
BEAR
HAIR
KING
HONEY
BEES
BOY

Across:

3. -
5. - LITTLE
6. - verg BIG
8. -
9. -
10.

Down:

1.
2.
3. sweet
4. hard
5.
7.
8.

```
Z V L U A S W K O F Z S D Z B G X X
Z F F Z J L A M I T Y D K I I O G A
D M A R B X H S V N X I E O V H Q I
P D C U U H U W K O G T K V G A Y O
D A N T K X O W N E H S E Y R W D G
G R A H J K H M O U D B L O V E J L
I L E N H M Z C E C E N I V K S H W
A R L I E E U U J I G A G R A I N A
N F G P I A Z S X M Q M I R F U X R
T C L E S I W U X I J E K I L V Q S
N K C H A R K Y D D X D C E T V O J
```

Look up and down for the words.
Have a good time searching.

Find these words in the letters above:

RUTH
LOVE   ASKED   WARS
HOME   NAME   SAUL
GLEAN   ARK   DAVID
GRAIN   KING   GIANT
                             WISE

Can you put these words in abc order?

THE STORY OF JONAH
A FISHY STORY

God told Jonah to go to the city of Nineveh. Jonah was to tell the people that the city was going to be destroyed. Jonah was afraid. He ran away. Jonah thought he could hide from God. He sailed on a ship. There was a terrible storm. All the men prayed for their lives. They threw their cargo overboard. But it did not help. Then the men found Jonah sound asleep in the ship. Jonah told them: "My God told me to tell the people they were going to be destroyed. I ran away. The storm is my fault. Throw me overboard and you will be safe. " So the sailors threw Jonah into the sea.

A great big whale swallowed Jonah. Inside the whale, Jonah asked God for forgiveness. He promised to obey God. God heard him. The fish threw Jonah onto the shore. Then Jonah went to Nineveh. He told the people that God was going to destroy the city. The people and the king changed their ways. God heard, and spared the city.

Jonah was angry with God. God saved the city when they repented. Why? Jonah went outside the city. During the night a large vine grew. It gave him shade from the sun. Then the vine died. Jonah cried. God asked if Jonah was sorry it was gone. Jonah said he was. If Jonah was sorry that a vine was destroyed, how would God feel if he had to kill an entire city of people? Now Jonah knew the wonder of God's love.

Connect the Dots

Connect the dots to find out what held Jonah.
Then have fun coloring.

ESTHER

SAVES HER PEOPLE

In the land of Persia, there was a king by the name of Ahasuerus. King Ahasuerus called for his queen. But she refused to go to him. The king was very angry. He had her killed. Now the king was looking for a new queen. All the girls made themselves ready. An Israelite, Mordecai, had a niece named Esther. He told her to go with the others. Maybe the king would choose her. And the king did choose beautiful Esther to be his queen.

One day, Mordecai overheard some men plotting to kill the king. He told Esther and Esther told the king. The king had these men killed. Now the King was very thankful to Mordecai.   The King wrote in his book that Mordecai had saved his life.

The wicked prime minister, Haman, did not like Mordecai. Mordecai would not bow down to him.   Haman told the king: "There are people in the kingdom who worship their own God. They should be killed." King Ahasuerus trusted Haman, so he agreed.

Mordecai heard this. He went to speak to Esther. She had to save her people.   Esther fasted and prayed. Then she went to see the king.   King Ahasuerus welcomed her.   She told him of a plot to kill the Jews in Persia. She told the king that she was an Israelite. This meant that she would be killed, too. The king realized that Haman was planning to kill his queen and Mordecai, who had saved his life. King Ahasuerus stopped the killing of the Jews. Then, the king ordered that evil Haman be hanged on the gallows instead.

What is it?

Color the different areas to find a full picture.
Use the guide below. What do you see in the picture?

Y- Yellow   G- Green   O- Orange   B- Brown

Wordsearch...

```
T T R U E F H W F M S L O P C O E W I
E Q E R H G O R P G G B O K L V Z H K
M X R D S E O E L A H W E Y F O V V H
P Y F N E T N K N Q S Z P H Q F T E H
L H A N G Q O I E N V D I I S W Q T A
E W D J F Q A R V S I T H D W B J S N
B N B J W L H W M D T L S E Z A Y A O
M O U B J X J L C M T H G G K Q L F J
S I S B J S Z C G V X I E P M K X L F
D L J N Q U E E N L E O Z R N R N W I
H A M A N S V J L T C X W J H D J C I
```

Look up and down and find the hidden words
listed below in the letters above.

Find these words in the letters above.

HIDE	TRUE	ESTHER
WHALE	WALL	JONAH
VINE	FAST	HAMAN
SHIP	HANG	PLOT
QUEEN	STORM	LION
	TEMPLE	

Can you put these words in abc order?

DANIEL
in the lions' den

Daniel was an important Israelite in King Belshazzar's kingdom. The king was bad. He did not follow the laws of God. One day, a hand appeared by a wall. It started writing on the wall in astrange language. "Mene, Mene, Tekel, Upharsin." Daniel understood the words. He told the king that the city would be invaded and conquered and it was.

The new king put Daniel in charge. The other leaders were jealous. They wanted to get him into trouble. They knew that Daniel worshipped God every day. So they went to the king and had him issue a decree: "For the next thirty days the people will worship only King Darius. Anyone worshipping another god will be thrown into the lions' den." That did not stop Daniel. He still worshipped his God three times a day.

The men told the king. Daniel was taken to the lions' den. King Darius prayed that Daniel's God would save him. All night long the king worried over Daniel's safety. In the morning, King Darius ran to the lions' den. Daniel was alive. Daniel said that God had sent an angel to protect him and shut the lions' mouths. Then the king had Daniel's accusers thrown into the lions' den. They were killed. King Darius declared Daniel's God a true God. He was the only God to worship from then on, throughout the kingdom.

Hidden Pictures

How many lions can you find in this picture?
Have fun coloring the picture.

FINAL TRIVIA

Clues on pages 56-57,60-61,66-67,70, 72-73,76-77,80,81,84,87,90

QUESTIONS

1. What did God give Moses to give to the people?
2. How did the people sin and what did they make?
3. What did Moses do when he came down from the mountain?
4. How many years did the people have to live in the desert?
5. Who led the people into the promised land?
6. How did God tell Joshua to conquer Jericho?
7. Who was a super stong leader of the people?
8. What happened when Samson's hair was cut?
9. What did Orpah and Ruth do when Naomi wanted to go home?
10. What was Saul looking for when he came to Samuel?
11. Whom did God have Samuel choose for a second king?
12. Whom did David fight with a slingshot?
13. Who was a very wise king?
14. After being thrown overboard, what carried Jonah?
15. How did God save Daniel?

ANSWERS

1) The Ten Commandments
2) A golden calf to worship
3) Broke the tablets
4) Forty (40)
5) Joshua
6) Circle the wall, make noise and blow the trumpets
7) Samson
8) He lost his strength
9) Orpah returned to her family and Ruth stayed with Naomi
10) His father's donkeys
11) David
12) The giant Goliath
13) Solomon
14) A big fish or whale
15) He sent an angel to protect him by closing the lions' mouths.

More Thoughts

Complete the sentences with your own answers.

1. I think the Ten Commandments are _____
_____.

2. If I were Moses, I _____
_____.

3. I think that Joshua_____
_____.

4. If I had Samson's strength, I_____
_____.

5. I think that Ruth and Naomi_____
_____.

6. If I had to fight a giant, I_____
_____.

7. I serve God when I_____
_____.

8. When I think of being as wise as King Solomon, I
_____.

9. The story of Jonah makes me think_____
_____.

10. I like the stories in the Bible because_____
_____.

ANSWERS

Page 7

```
H T R A E A S G S L G P Z A Y N H
S I G R J N U U H O I O A F G R E
B S N D O I N B X C S G E C X I A
I E J N D M N O O M S A H B X C V
N S A A W A U D U I G K E T X G E
M E S R M L V Y V S U A Y S O Y N
O V O B H S P N H T S W D F X Z J
Y E A Y S T O R I E S S O A Y S A
C E B T E F C A Q B O O Z K F X O
Z B H O A I X I Q A U Z Y W Q M R
Y V E U G R D J G C W U P E E B Y
```

Page 14

A-MAZING

Find your way throught the maze of animals and rooms on the ark until you find Noah's room. Enter through the door.

ENTER →

Page 27

```
I E L B Y E B O A T W L E R W
D S Y T S U U N A T E U Q B A
M A T E O D M N V S N S E A D
M R M W N L G K H O T E T B Z
A A A M O T S L O D I A T Y R
N H D P I H V P F V Q V R D E
Y S Z A T S L E G N A I E S T
Q Q X B A P R A Y L Z I S U A
Y K N D N K B S P K N O G D W
R B P J L I V E P Z F N O L R
```

Page 17

```
                                1
                                M
                    2       3
                    W       S T A R S
            5       O       N
        4   T W O   M       A
        B       O   B A R K E
    6           W       N
    B E A R     N
        7
        A P P L E N
        I       R
    10
    S U N
```

Page 31

MAZE

Find your way from the well with water for all ten camels.

START WELL

END

Page 19

```
V M F U X Q P R A Y T B V C R J O E
Y V R I C S Q H E W T W O A B B B U
A D U J M P I Y J S F W J D A G S F
R I I A I S S G M Y N Q F A B T R F
K V T H B N R D A U M F S M E O T V
U U L A A E I K D F E V E K L Y O S
E L P P A O L A A D E Y B H Y M W S
K L S B I X N N R W U E E T Q T E O
Z L T A R O S B T K A L R F V C R I
R X V Q T P C A I N S H Z T M R F Q
T Y M A U U C I D O L S Z O T K N B
```

Page 23

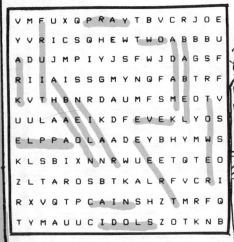

miracle MAZE

Find your way through the evil city of Sodom. Help Lot's family get out of the city before it is destroyed.

SAFETY

Page 34

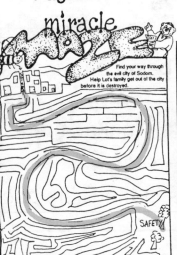

```
E V X L X U A H C K A I G L D X F V
B A B Y L B B C J C D O I I O E A Y
F H Z K W E R B N Q W T Y R F P T R
O O S P N W S I B Z V O G B W T C L
O L K B Q X S G D C H L V N O Q S O
T B I A W I F E T E K E S I T Y O V
E W N H L J O R A E C F N U I X S E
U G Q L M N P P K R G O I O I C T T
G E T R I C K W F U H O W R K I N E
O W K X Y M M M S B N D T L L E W C
```

ANSWERS

Page 38

Page 39

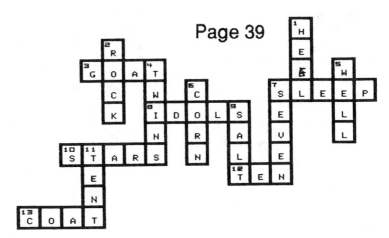

Page 43

Page 50

Page 62

Page 63

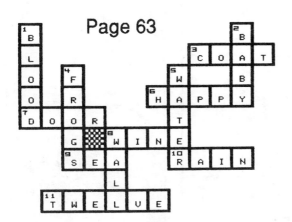

Page 68

Hidden Pictures

How many frogs can you find?

ANSWERS

Page 69

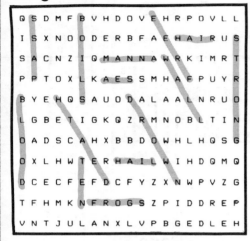

```
Q S D M F B V H D O V E H R P O V L L
I S X N O O D E R B F A E H A I R U S
S A C N Z I Q M A N N A W R K I M R T
P P T O X L K A E S S M H A F P U Y R
B Y E H Q S A U O D A L A A L N R U O
L G B E T I G K Q Z R M N O B L T I N
O A D S C A H X B B D O W H L H Q S G
O X L H W T E R H A I L W I H D Q M Q
D C E C F E F D C F Y Z X N W P V Z G
T F H M K N F R O G S Z P I D D R E P
V N T J U L A N X L V P B G E D L E H
```

Page 74

Page 79

Page 82

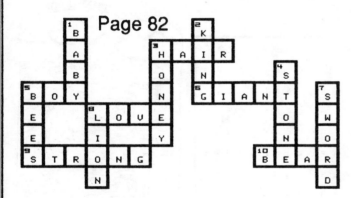

Page 83

```
Z V L U A S W K O F Z S D Z B G X X
Z F F Z J L A M I T Y D K I I O G A
D M A R B X H S V N X I E O V H Q I
P D C U U H U W K O G T K V G A Y O
D A N T K X O W N E H S E Y R W D G
G R A H J K H M O U D B L O V E J L
I L E N H M Z C E C E N I V K S H W
A R L I E E U U J I G A G R A I N A
N F G P I A Z S X M Q M I R F U X R
T C L E S I W U X I J E K I L V Q S
N K C H A R K Y D D X D C E T V O J
```

Page 85

Page 89

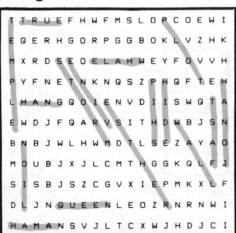

```
T T R U E F H W F M S L O P C O E W I
E Q E R H G O R P G G B O K L V Z H K
M X R D S E O E L A H W E Y F O V V H
P Y F N E T N K N Q S Z P H Q F T E H
L H A N G Q O I E N V D I I S W Q T A
E W D J F Q A R V S I T H D W B J S N
B N B J W L H W M D T L S E Z A Y A O
M O U B J X J L C M T H G G K Q L F J
S I S B J S Z C G V X I E P M K X L F
D L J N Q U E E N L E O Z R N R N W I
H A M A N S V J L T C X W J H D J C I
```

Page 91